THE ULTIMATE EMOJi STICKER ACTIVITY BOOK

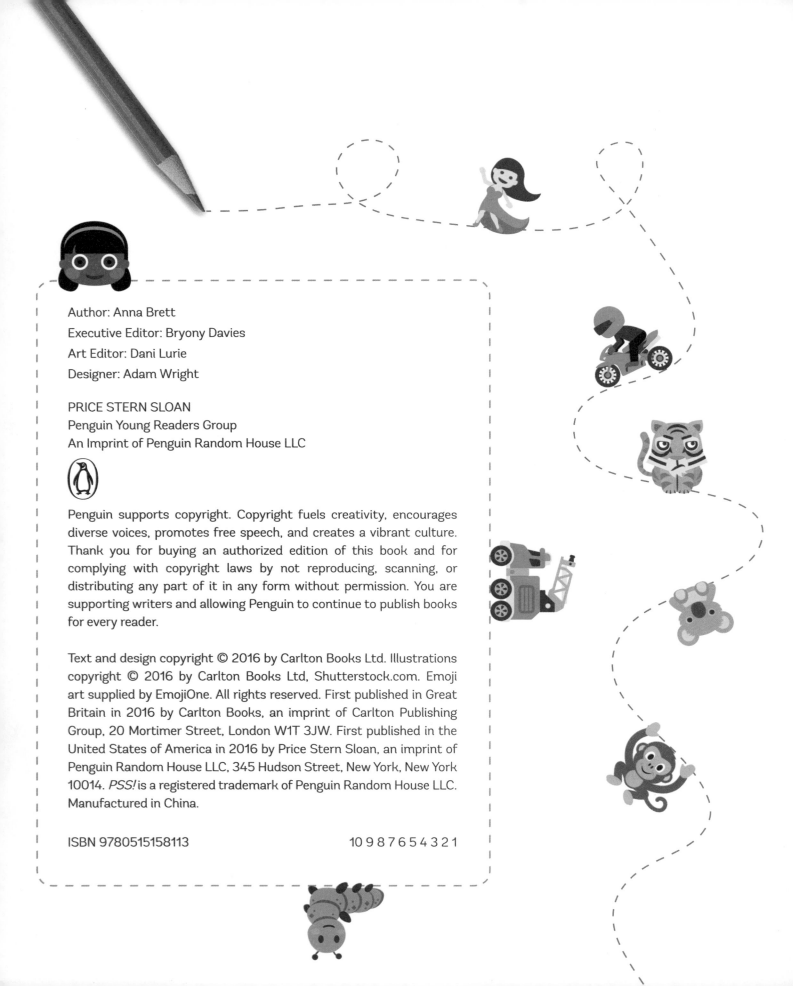

Author: Anna Brett

Executive Editor: Bryony Davies

Art Editor: Dani Lurie

Designer: Adam Wright

PRICE STERN SLOAN
Penguin Young Readers Group
An Imprint of Penguin Random House LLC

Text and design copyright © 2016 by Carlton Books Ltd. Illustrations copyright © 2016 by Carlton Books Ltd, Shutterstock.com. Emoji art supplied by EmojiOne. All rights reserved. First published in Great Britain in 2016 by Carlton Books, an imprint of Carlton Publishing Group, 20 Mortimer Street, London W1T 3JW. First published in the United States of America in 2016 by Price Stern Sloan, an imprint of Penguin Random House LLC, 345 Hudson Street, New York, New York 10014. *PSS!* is a registered trademark of Penguin Random House LLC. Manufactured in China.

ISBN 9780515158113   10 9 8 7 6 5 4 3 2 1

THE ULTIMATE EMOJI STICKER ACTIVITY BOOK

PSS!
PRICE STERN SLOAN
AN IMPRINT OF PENGUIN RANDOM HOUSE

Top ten emojis

Everyone has their personal favorite emojis, and at certain times of the year, particular icons peak (we're looking at you, Santa!), but here are the top ten most commonly used emojis on Twitter.

TWITTER TOP 10

Do you agree or disagree with this list? Stick your top five emojis here. You'll find them on the sticker pages:

1

2

3

4

5

Emoji bingo

You are now entering a world of emojis. And once you start, you won't be able to stop spotting these little characters everywhere. So why not make a game out of it and play emoji bingo!

1 The goal of emoji bingo is to cross out five emojis in a line (vertically, horizontally, or diagonally) in each grid. The grid you complete first is the winner.

2 The three grids you see on page seven are the three games you'll be playing.

Grid 1 — Text message emoji bingo
Grid 2 — Out and about emoji bingo
Grid 3 — The "Emoji Sticker Activity Book" emoji bingo

3 Grid 1 is a game based on the text messages you receive from your friends. Whenever someone sends you an emoji that appears in the grid you're allowed to cross it out. Remember, you have to get five in a row to complete the game.

4 Grid 2 is a game based on the emojis you encounter in everyday life! Spot a smiley face at school? Cross it out on the grid!

5 Grid 3 is a game based on the activities in this book. Work your way from beginning to end and every time you spot one of the emojis shown in the grid you are allowed to cross it out.

6 You'll notice there's a free square in each grid. This is a freebie to help you complete a line, so don't forget it. **Game on!**

Grid 1

Text message emoji bingo

 FREE

Grid 2

Out and about emoji bingo

 FREE

Grid 3

The "Emoji Sticker Activity Book" emoji bingo

 FREE

Emoji events

You can use emojis to represent almost every event and national holiday.

Write down what event the emojis represent in the list below.

1. 🎂 ← ....

2. .... → 🍂

3. 🎓 ← ....

4. .... → 🍀

5. 💘 ← ....

6. .... → 🎅

7. 🐉 ← ....

Now place the emoji sticker that you think is the best fit next to each of these events.

8 .... ← Wedding

9 Father's Day →

10 .... ← Halloween

11 Independence Day →

12 .... ← Mother's Day

13 Super Bowl →

14 .... ← Bastille Day

Answer at the back of the book.

Emoji-doku

Sudoku can be brain-twistingly difficult and even frustrating at times, but these emojis have done some of the hard work for you!

Stick the correct faces in the squares so that each row, column, and mini-grid of four contains only one of each emoji. You'll find the emojis on the sticker pages.

PUZZLE 1

PUZZLE 2

Answer at the back of the book.

Underwater oddity

Life underwater is great for these emojis. The water is warm, the fish are friendly—but hang on, can you spot something out of place?

Answer at the back of the book.

It's cold out there!

Everyone is having fun on the slopes today. The weather is cold but the snow is fresh and fun! There's something growing here that doesn't belong. Can you spot it?

EmojiLand

Answer at the back of the book.

Flags and countries

Can you name the countries these emoji flags belong to?

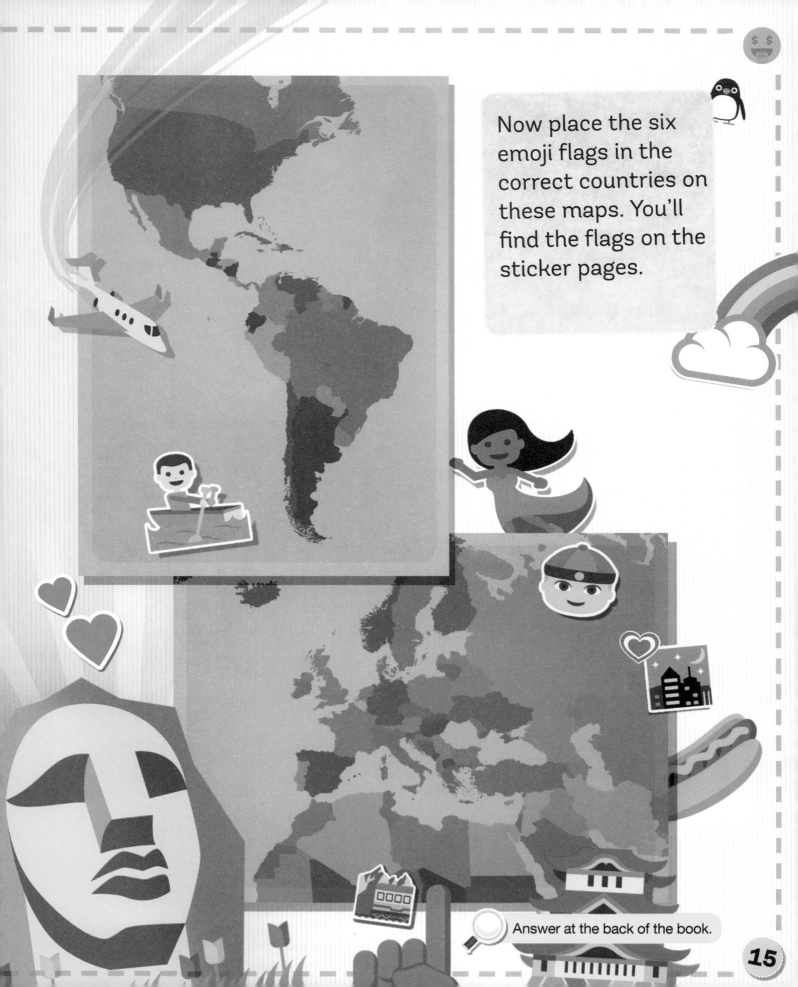

Now place the six emoji flags in the correct countries on these maps. You'll find the flags on the sticker pages.

Answer at the back of the book.

15

Dinnertime!

Mr. Wolf eats his dinner at 7 o'clock sharp every evening! Can you solve these emoji time-themed puzzles? You can write in the answers for questions one and three, and use stickers from the sticker pages for questions two and four.

1 On Monday, Mr. Wolf ate his lunch at 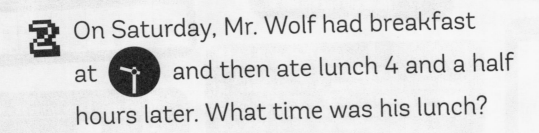 and then had dinner at . How long did he wait between meals?

....

2 On Saturday, Mr. Wolf had breakfast at and then ate lunch 4 and a half hours later. What time was his lunch?

3 On Sunday, Mr. Wolf was lazy and had a late brunch. After brunch, his next meal was dinner, at his usual time of 7pm. If brunch was at 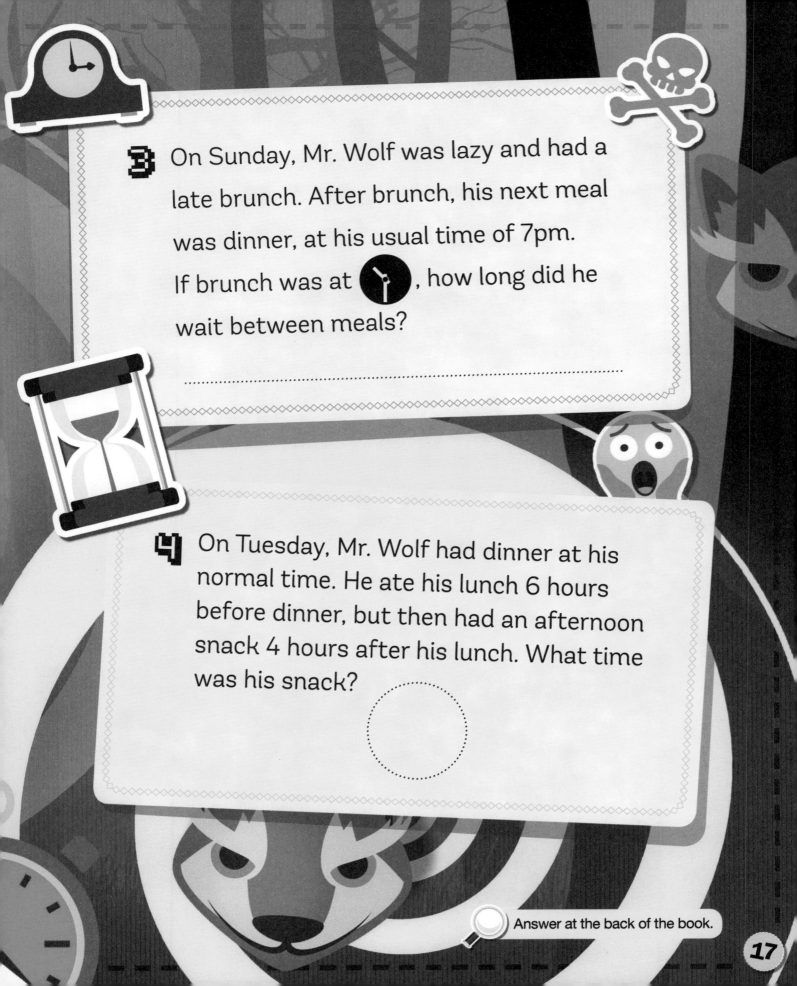, how long did he wait between meals?

....

4 On Tuesday, Mr. Wolf had dinner at his normal time. He ate his lunch 6 hours before dinner, but then had an afternoon snack 4 hours after his lunch. What time was his snack?

Answer at the back of the book.

Munch maze

Navigate the munch maze, avoiding the ghosts and gobbling up all the watermelon slices along the way.

ENTRANCE

EXIT

Answer at the back of the book.

Emoji-search

Can you spot the following emoji sequences in the grid below?
They can appear horizontally or vertically.

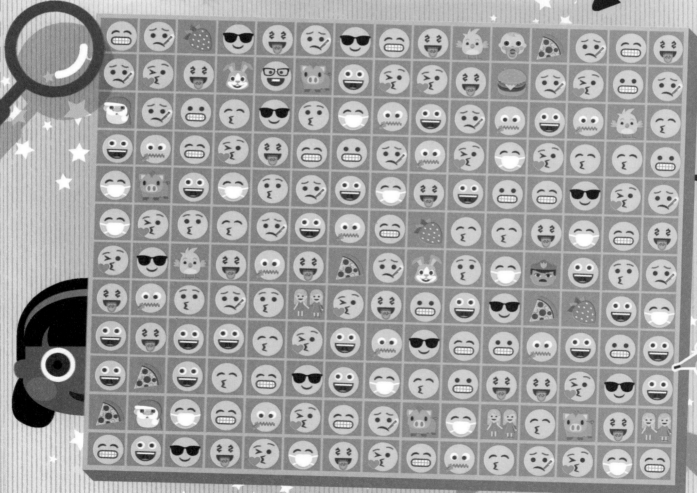

Answer at the back of the book.

Turn the page to discover what to do with this brilliant emoji mask!

Glue Popsicle stick here

Emoji masks

Emoji masks are so much fun!
Cut them out and off you go!

Glue the end of the Popsicle stick to the bottom of the back of the mask. Use it to hold up the mask in front of your face.

What you'll need:

- A pair of small scissors
- A Popsicle stick (eat the Popsicle first!)
- A glue stick
- An adult—for supervision!

If you get too hot running around with your emoji mask on, use it as a fan to cool yourself down!

Count the crocs

How many crocodiles can you count in this green emoji scene?

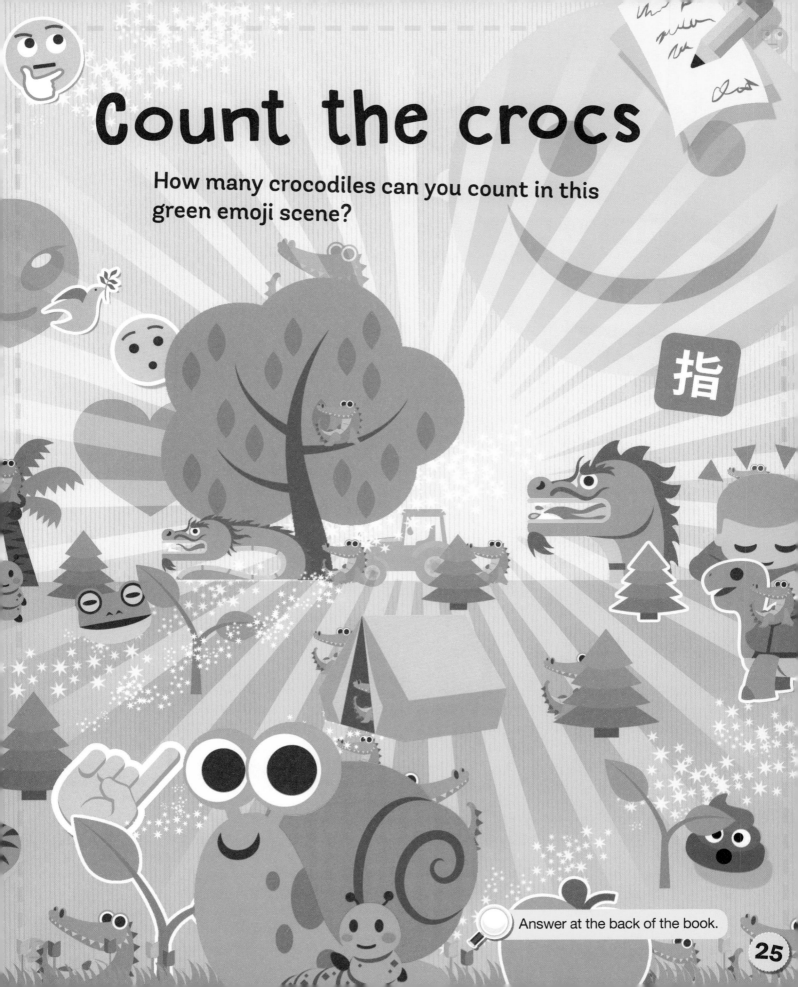

Answer at the back of the book.

Emoji history

History can be confusing, especially with all those dates and people's names and places. Let's emojify history to make it fun to remember and difficult to forget!

Let's put your world knowledge to the test! Let's try one together...

MAN MAN SEE BIRD IDEA BUILD PLANE

= The Wright brothers' first flight, 1903!

Now it's your turn. Can you solve these emoji events?

1

....

2

....

3

....

4

....

5

....

GIVE IT A GO!

Now it's your turn to come up with three world history events. Think of a historical moment, find stickers from the sticker pages that work, and stick them in the correct order below. See if your friends or family can guess the event correctly!

....

....

....

 Answer at the back of the book.

Emoji family album!

We play, send, and receive so many emojis every day that we've gotten to know their cute little yellow faces just as well as we do our own family!

Place the emoji sticker on top of the head that you feel best sums up the family members below.

Complete these picture frames with emoji faces, then make up a name for each portrait.

Weather forecast

Did you know the idea for emojis came from the symbols weather forecasters use on their maps?

Stick the appropriate emojis on these weather maps.

There will be sunshine and showers today in the south of England and London.

Caution! Tornado warning for Texas in the southern United States of America.

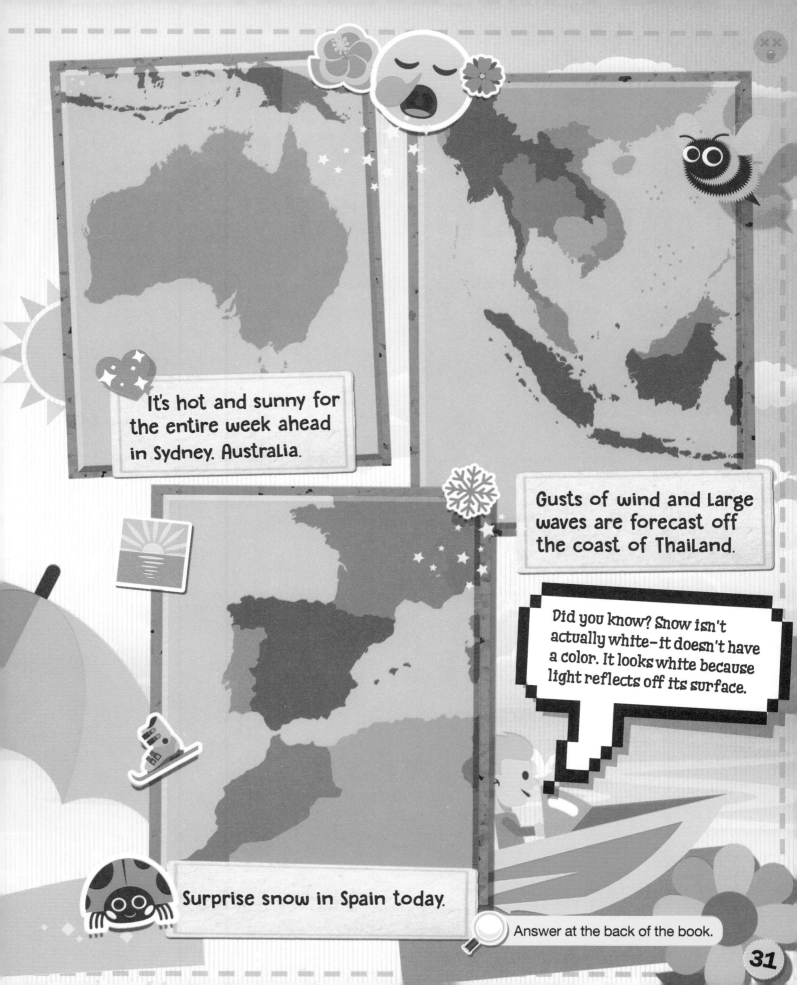

It's hot and sunny for the entire week ahead in Sydney, Australia.

Gusts of wind and large waves are forecast off the coast of Thailand.

Did you know? Snow isn't actually white—it doesn't have a color. It looks white because light reflects off its surface.

Surprise snow in Spain today.

Answer at the back of the book.

Design your own emojis

There are over 1,600 emojis, but there's always room for a few more.

Grab a pencil and design away...

Draw a new face.

Create an emoji for a sport that doesn't have one yet.

Show your favorite food.

Design a new way to get around!

Emoji zoo

There are lots of cute (and not so cute!) emoji animals. Fill this zoo with weird and wonderful emoji creatures.

- 😀 Who lives in the water?
- 😊 Which animals will you choose to live together in one area?
- 😬 Has anything escaped from its enclosure?

Emoji sports day

It's the first day of the International Emoji Games and the competitors are gathering for the opening ceremony. They have to register their sport with the officials.

Can you work out which events the athletes are competing in? Stick the correct emoji from the sticker pages alongside each sport's description.

I play a team sport that is hugely popular around the whole world. All I need is a → round ball and two goals to start the game.

Shoot some hoops with me—just
← grab the orange ball to begin.

I play a racket sport. The object I hit over →
the high net is very light and made of feathers.

My goal is to hit a small ball into 18 holes
← around a course using the fewest strokes possible.

I don't need much gear for this sport. In fact, the less the better! Goggles are required to help me see, though. →

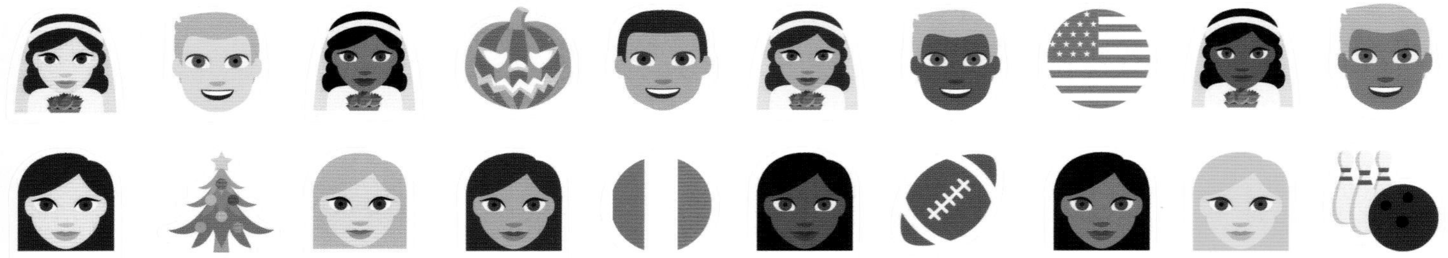

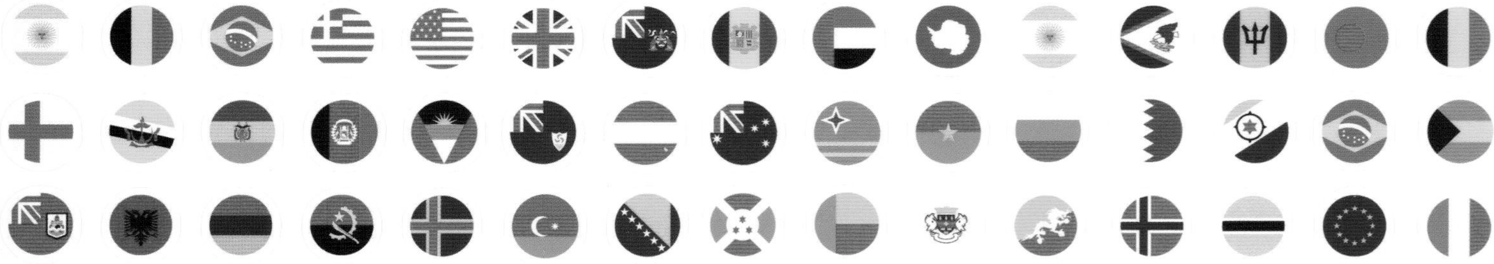

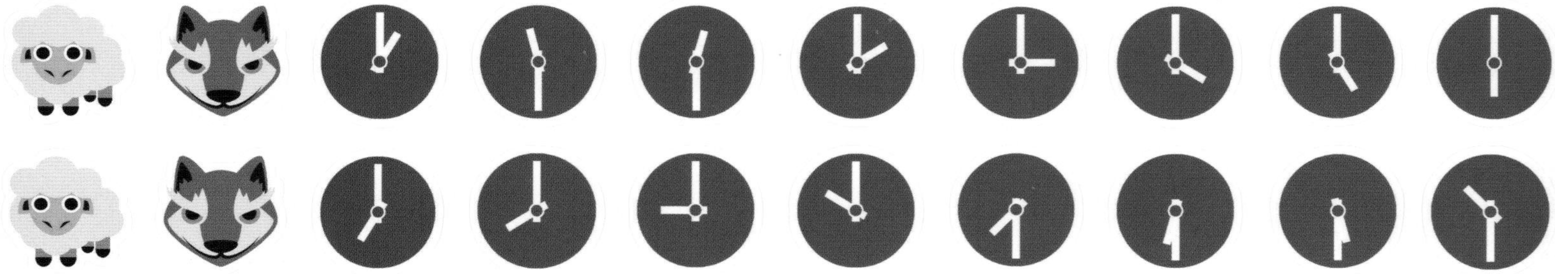

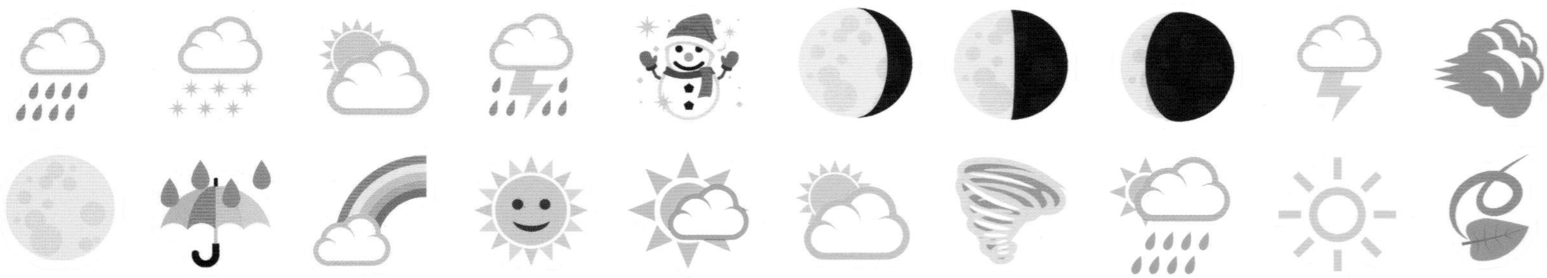

Pages 48-49

Pages 50-51

Page 66

Pages 68-69

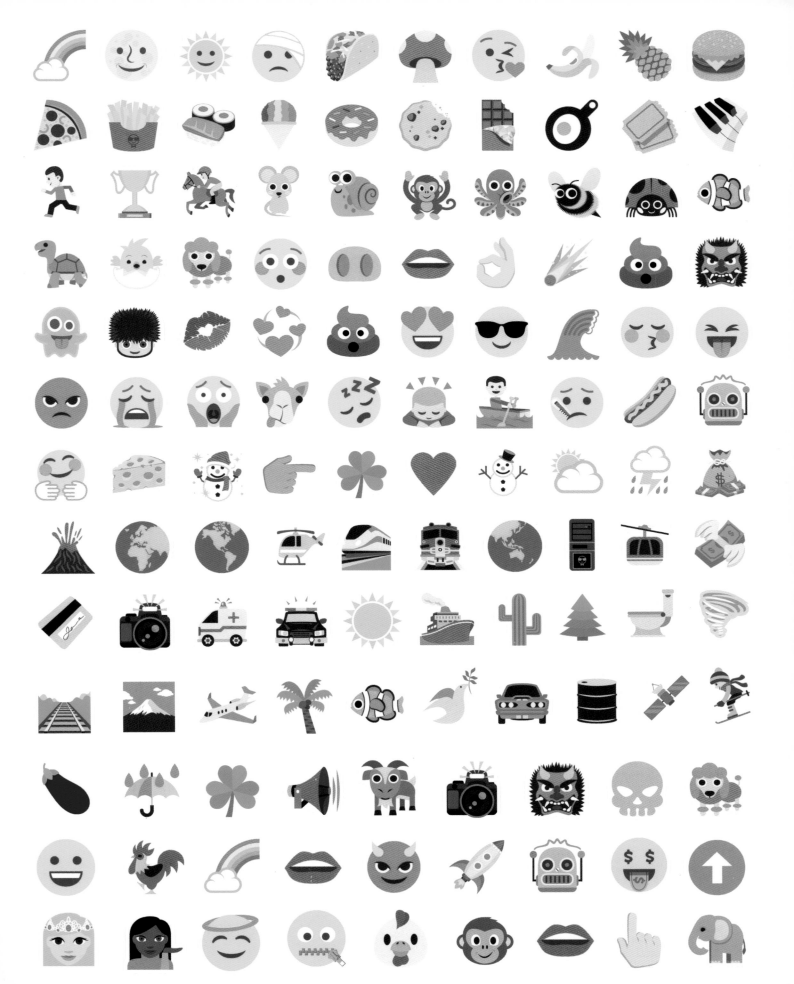

My sport requires two team members.
← One is a human and the other is an animal. We run and jump together.

Unlike many sports, the goal of my game is to stay very still and not wobble when holding → my equipment. With any luck I'll hit the center of the target.

My sport takes place in the winter because I
← need snow to compete. My feet are strapped to a board.

Pick it up, lift it high, win the gold medal! It's a simple strategy but I need strong → muscles to win the event!

I play on a court with a racket and
← a ball. I can either play outdoors or indoors.

Answer at the back of the book.

Name that film

Can you work out the names of these famous films by decoding the emojis?

Here's one to try together:

A baby and a bear, snake, tiger, and elephant...

Lots of plants and trees and a book!
It must be: **THE JUNGLE BOOK.**

The emojis below describe each film's content, characters, or storyline. Write your answer below each set of clues.

See if you can work these out!

1

....

2

....

Guess the odd emoji out

Think you know your emojis by now? See if you can spot which of these is not actually an emoji. Circle the odd emoji in each line.

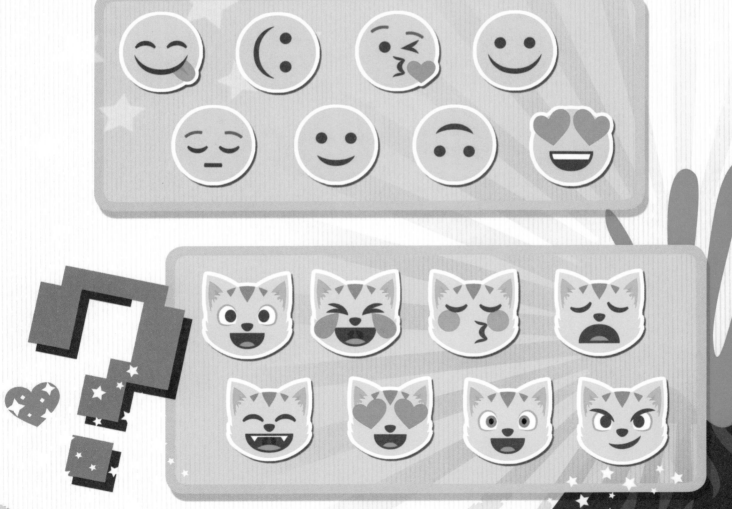

 Answer at the back of the book.

Emoji-merge

Create your own emojis by merging the features of the two we've suggested!

Emoji-tastes

Do you prefer sweet or savory, or do your taste buds like to be surprised? Answer these questions to reveal your favorites.

1 It's movie night and Mom says you can choose the snacks. Do you go for:

A B  C

2 Which of these is your favorite fruit?

A  B C

3 For breakfast, you love a good plate of:

A  B   C

4 It's your birthday! You ask for a special platter of:

A  B C

5 Your favorite meal is:

A  B C

6 If you could only eat one vegetable for the rest of your life it would be:

A B C

7 You have to give up one of these food groups forever. Would you choose:

A B C

8 What's your favourite type of meat?

A B C

9 Would you rather eat:

A B C

10 You're making a three-course feast for your family. What would you cook? Circle one item from each column.

A B C

A B C

A B C

Mostly As –
You've got sensible tastes and are a healthy eater. Well done!

Mostly Bs –
You love food and the sweeter the better. Remember to brush your teeth regularly!

Mostly Cs –
You'll try anything and think outside the box when it comes to flavor combinations. Maybe you'll be a famous chef when you grow up!

45

Connect three

Grab a friend and play this game with the red and blue emoji circle stickers.

Instructions

☻ - Decide who is playing with red and who is playing with blue.

☻ - Toss a coin to see who gets to start first.

☻ - Player one should place a sticker of their color over one of the circles in the bottom row of the grid.

☻ - Player two can now place their sticker somewhere on the bottom row of the grid, or in the circle above player one's sticker.

☻ - Continue taking turns to place the stickers but remember, you can only work from the bottom up so you must place your sticker on the bottom row, or in the circle above another sticker.

☻ - The goal of the game is to get three of your stickers in a row before the other player. You can make lines horizontally, vertically, or diagonally.

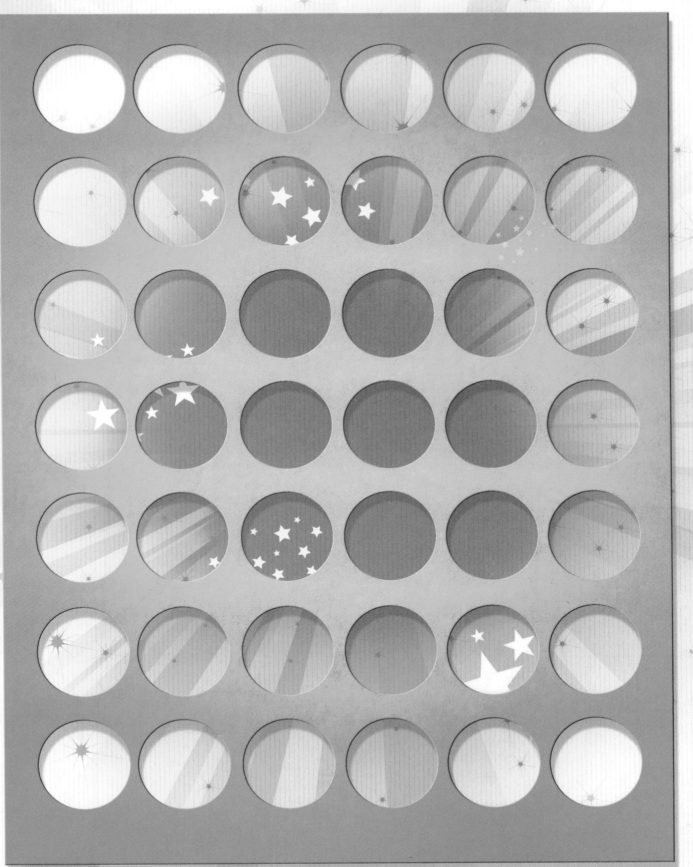

Card game

Here are a few playing cards from a standard emoji card pack. Some of the symbols on the cards are missing. Look carefully, and use your emoji suit stickers to complete all the cards.

Answer at the back of the book.

Where does the emoji come from?

Do you know where these emojis come from? Find them on the sticker sheet and stick them on the country or region you think they originate from.

 Hint — It might look like the Eiffel Tower but it's not! This one's in Japan. ←

 Hint — It's not Hollywood, it begins with a B and it's much farther east. ←

 Hint — This thirsty fellow lives in the Sahara Desert. →

Answer at the back of the book.

Name that book!

Can you work out the name of the book by decoding the emojis? We've given you each author name as a clue!

Author: Eric Carle

1 ....

Author: E. B. White

2 ....

Author: Robert Louis Stevenson

3 ....

Author: Roald Dahl

4 ....

Author: Antoine de Saint-Exupéry

5 ....

Author: Roald Dahl

6 ....

Author: Lewis Carroll

7 ....

Author: Jules Verne

8 ....

Answer at the back of the book.

53

Color-oji

Grab your pens, pencils, paints, and crayons and color in these emojis.

Will you match the original emoji colors or create your own design?

Emoji-search

Can you spot the following emoji sequences in the grid below?

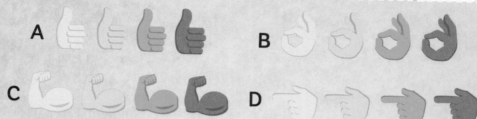

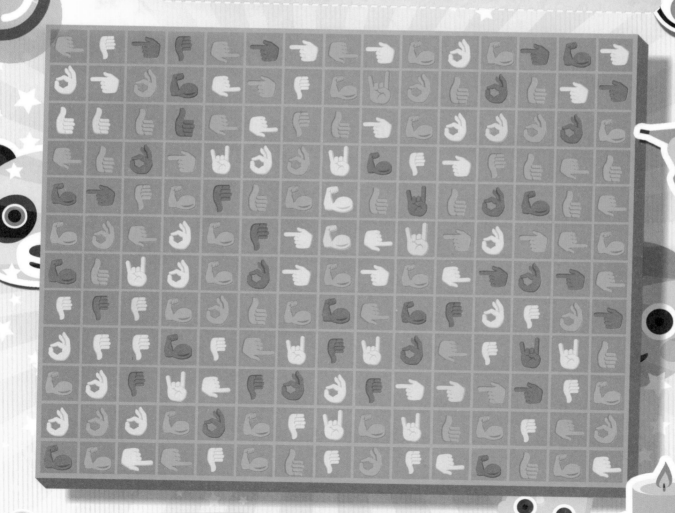

Answer at the back of the book.

Emoji door hangers

Emojis are all about showing how you feel with an image, so what better than an emoji door hanger to let people know if they are welcome in your room or not!

Just cut out this shape!

HEY, IT'S COOL, YOU'RE TOTALLY WELCOME TO COME IN!

Choose which side best displays your mood, and hang it with that side out on your bedroom door handle.

STAY OUT OF MY WAY TODAY!

Design your own emoji-tee

Decorate this T-shirt with your favorite emojis. You can draw them on or add stickers from the sticker pages.

Sign Language

There are over 20 hand emojis, but do you know what they all mean? Untangle the lines to find out some of the more difficult ones.

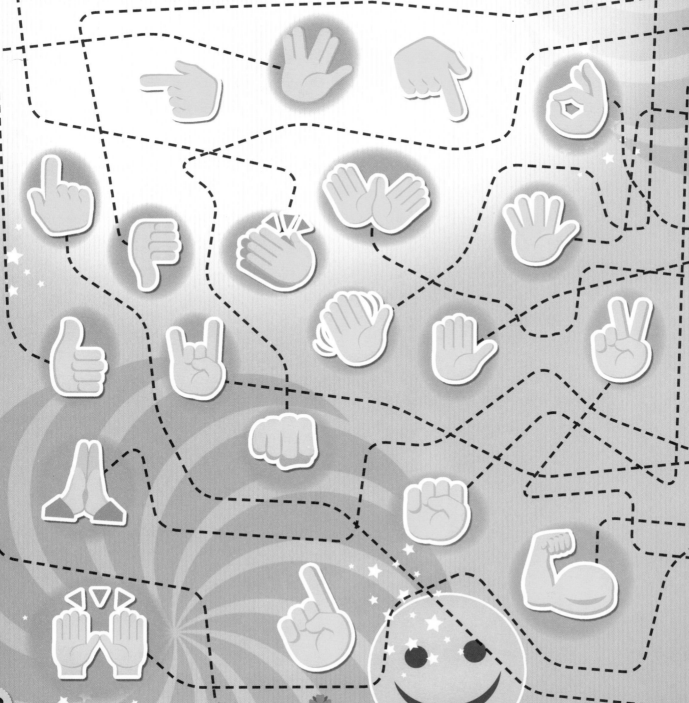

😃 **Clapping hands**

😃 **Waving hand**

😃 **Thumb up** (good)

😃 **Thumb down** (bad)

😃 **Fisted hand** (punch–bad, or fist-bump–good!)

😃 **Raised fist** (fist-pump)

😃 **Folded hands** (means please or thank you in Japanese but people also use it to signify praying or a high-five)

😃 **Pointing up index finger** (represents the number one)

😃 **OK hand sign** (OK or yes, that's correct)

😃 **Raised hand** (stop or a high-five)

😃 **Open hands** (means openness but sometimes used as a hug or jazz hands)

😃 **Both hands raised** (celebration)

😃 **Raised hand with fingers splayed** (the number five)

😃 **Sign of the horns** ("rock on")

😃 **Raised hand with gap between middle and ring finger** (a Star Trek symbol that means "live long and prosper")

😃 **Flexed bicep** (strength or meaning to work out)

😃 **Victory hand** (also known as the peace symbol)

What does it mean?

Because emojis originated in Japan, you may not know what some of the symbols mean unless you speak Japanese!

Here are some simple translations. Try drawing the characters out alongside the emojis to help you remember them.

Can you write a simple sentence using these emojis?

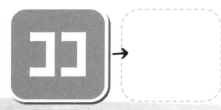 →

Means "here," referring to a destination.

 →

Means "moon" or "month."

 →

Means to "own" or "possess."

 →

Means "a good bargain."

 →

Symbol for a sale, meaning "to cut prices."

 →

Means "prohibit," "restrict," or "forbid."

 →

Means "request" in Japanese. In Chinese it means "monkey" in the Chinese zodiac!

合 →

Means "agreement" or more literally, to unite or join together.

空 →

Means "empty" and "available," in the context of a parking space or hotel room.

祝 →

Means "congratulations."

秘 →

Means "secret."

満 →

Means "full" in terms of full capacity.

営 →

Means "work."

無 →

Means to "lack" or "have none of."

A Japanese man called Shigetaka Kurita invented the first set of emojis!

Emoji day spa

Pick the best emoji stickers to illustrate this day spa menu of treatments.

Welcome to the Emoji day spa

Relax and let us pamper you in our deluxe salon. Treatments include:

Haircut
We know it's important for emojis to have good hair. Join us for a cut or color. We use top-quality scissors and offer a "hair back" policy if you don't like what we've cut off!

Manicure
Orange is the color of the moment for your nails, so make an appointment for your manicure soon!

Pucker up
This is a special offer for all those emojis who love to kiss–come in for a color session and we'll pick out the lipstick shade that's perfect for you. Mwah!

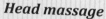

Head massage
Feeling stressed from all those messages you need to reply to? Headache from too much time spent on your phone? We emojis know it's tough out there so come in now for a relaxing head massage.

Full-body massage
Ease away those aches and pains with a full-body massage. We now offer a double hand massage for all our loyal emojis.

Hot springs spa bath
Learn how to take a bath the emoji way. Extra-special triple steam means you'll cleanse the air around you as well as your skin. This treatment can be enjoyed indoors or out in our moveable bathtubs.

Bridal package
Let us get you ready for your big day! Hair, nails, and makeup are standard, and if you include a **Pucker up** treatment we'll throw in three red roses for free!

Read them aLL!

How many books can you count in this pile?
Write your answer at the bottom of the page.

Answer at the back of the book.

Music mistake

It's time for the band to go onstage but they've lost their sheet music! They are trying to remember the song and have noted down who needs to play when.

Look at the sequence and fill in the gaps using your stickers.

Helpful hints

☻ -The chorus, which is the green line, is repeated 3 times.
It's always the same sequence of instruments.
☻ -The piano always plays.
☻ -The singer and saxophone always perform at the same time.
☻ -The guitar always plays after the violin.

CHORUS

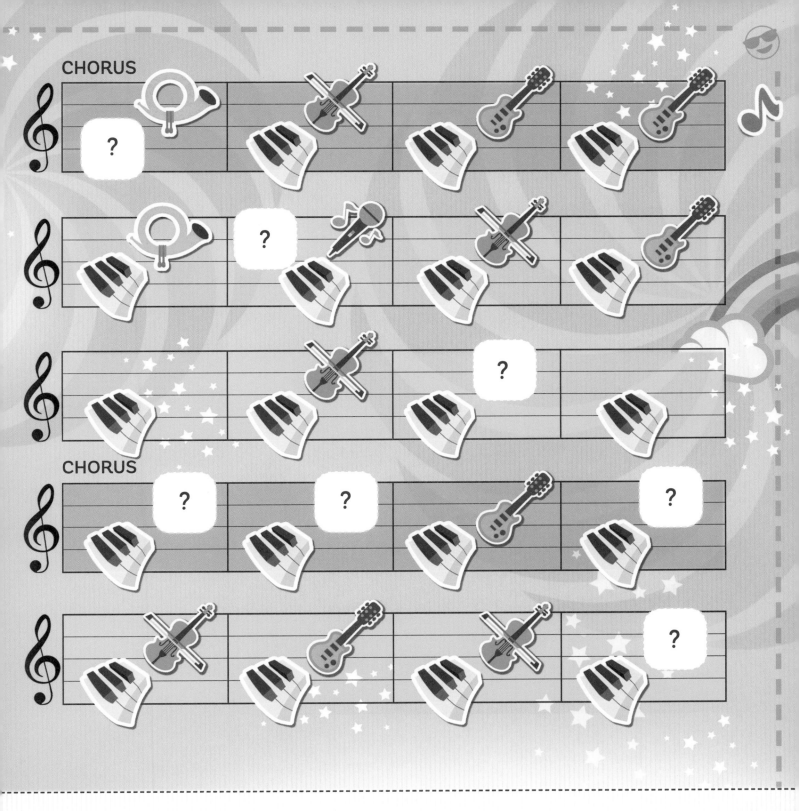

See page 70 for instructions about this area!

Game time!

You can play this game with two to four players, all you'll need is a dice.

First, cut out the four emoji faces at the bottom of this page and pick the one you would like to use as your game piece. Ask your friends to choose their own emoji face.

To play the game:

- All players should take a turn rolling the dice. The player with the highest number goes first.

- Player 1 should roll the dice and then move his or her game piece the correct number of spaces along the board.

- Players take turns, aiming to be the first to reach square number 80.

- To win the game, you have to land on square 80 exactly. If you roll too high a number, move back into the game board after reaching 80.

- Some emojis are good and some are bad! They might help you along or send you backwards.

← **Game faces** →